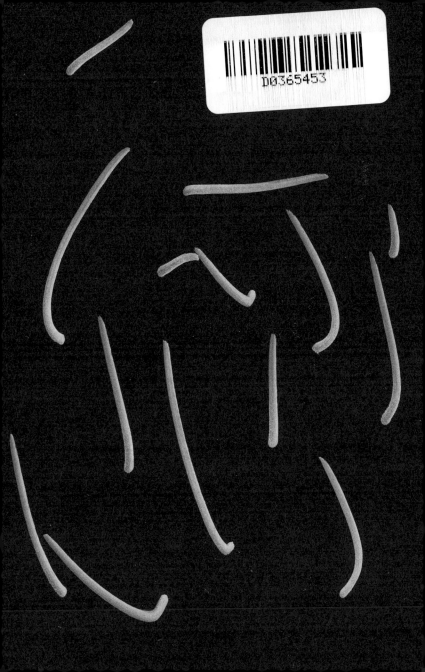

Where
Love Is,
There God
Is Also

Leo
Tolstoy

Where
Love Is,
There God
Is Also

Compiled by Lawrence Jordan

Fleming H. Revell
A Division of Baker Book House Co
Grand Rapids, Michigan 49516

© 1993, 2001 by Morning Star Rising, Inc.

Published by Fleming H. Revell
a division of Baker Book House Company
P.O. Box 6287, Grand Rapids, MI 49516-6287

Printed in the United States of America

Library of Congress Cataloging-in-Publication Data

Tolstoy, Leo, graf, 1828–1910.
  [Short stories. English. Selections]
    Where love is, there God is also / Leo Tolstoy.
      p.   cm.
    Contents: Where love is, there God is also—The three hermits—What men live by.
    ISBN 0-8007-1781-3 (cloth)
    1. Tolstoy, Leo, graf, 1828–1910—Translations into English.
  2. Christian fiction, Russian—Translations into English. I. Title.
PG3366.A13 D65   2001
891.73'3—dc21   00-064041

For current information about all releases from Baker Book House, visit our web site:
http://www.bakerbooks.com

Contents

Acknowledgments

All of the stories in this collection were translated by Nathan Haskell Dole.

I am indebted to the Library of Congress for courtesies extended to me. I am grateful to Diane Venora, who first read Tolstoy to me, and to Mae Sakharov, who among my friends was the first to discover Tolstoy's Christian stories.

I am especially indebted to A. N. Wilson, whose magnificent biography of Tolstoy was so helpful to me as I wrote an introduction to this collection. For anyone wishing to understand Tolstoy the man, the writer, the Christian artist, and his times, Wilson's biography is must reading. However, the conclusions I drew from the material on Tolstoy that A. N. Wilson so compellingly presented were not the same as those drawn by Wilson.

Introduction

Every good and perfect gift is from above, coming down from the Father of the heavenly lights, who does not change like shifting shadows.

James 1:17 NIV

I first became aware of Leo Tolstoy's Christian stories one winter Sunday afternoon when an actress friend of mine invited me to a reading after church. Her final selection was Tolstoy's "Where Love Is, There God Is Also," the story of an old cobbler who, because he believes what the gospel says is true, tries to live as the Lord instructs us to live and waits expectantly for a visit from Christ. Hearing this straightforward, seemingly simplistic tale deeply touched something in me and everyone else in the room that day. I had never heard the story before, and I was shocked that it was written by Tolstoy.

"Where Love Is, There God Is Also" started an intense inquisitiveness in me to find out more about this man and to read as many of his Christian works as possible. My friend loaned me her book, and my odyssey with Tolstoy's gospel stories began. What I discovered was that while many of his nonfiction religious works were in print, very few of his short fiction works with Christian themes were available. The more I researched, collected, and read, the more astonishing it became to me that these stories are largely unknown to today's Christians. The modern Christian world did not know Tolstoy's gospel stories as a part of its heritage.

Then I started to read more about Tolstoy's life, and it became clear to me in a flood why, at least in part, this was so.

Tolstoy. Perhaps the first images that come to mind at the very mention of his name are the great novels *War and Peace* and *Anna Karenina.* But there is a Tolstoy virtually unknown to the modern reader, a Tolstoy more intensely interested and concerned with things spiritual than his two great novels indicate, a Tolstoy for whom the most important aspect of life was one's relationship with God. The three stories in this collection are the products of this Tolstoy.

Introduction

Who was this man? Was he a Christian? And, most importantly, does his work have spiritual relevance for our day?

Lev Nikolayevich Tolstoy was born on August 28, 1828, and he died on November 7, 1910. Unlike many great writers, Tolstoy was not born poor or middle class. He was born into a wealthy family of the highest social class of Russian society, but one that was not very rich by the Russian standards of his day.

Tolstoy never really knew his mother, who died when he was two. His father died when Tolstoy was nine, leaving five children—four boys and a girl—orphans. Being a child of privilege without parents had a profound influence on Tolstoy. He would forever be both a part of and an outsider to the societies he was to inhabit. Here is an early self-assessment:

> What am I? One of four sons of a retired lieutenant-colonel, left an orphan at [nine] years of age in the care of women and strangers, having received neither a social nor an academic education and becoming my own master at the age of seventeen, without a large fortune, without any social position, without, above all, my principles.[1]

Tolstoy also described himself as "ugly, awkward, untidy, and socially uneducated." This young man developed enormous gifts and powers of observation and imagination, largely through voracious reading and the almost daily diary he started as a young man and kept for most of his life.

In 1869 at the age of forty-one, Tolstoy finished *War and Peace,* the novel called "the greatest masterpiece in prose fiction."[2] Eight years later, in April 1877, he finished *Anna Karenina.* From this point until the end of his life—for the next thirty-three years—Tolstoy would be overwhelmingly preoccupied with the things of the spirit in both his fiction and nonfiction writing.

Most commentators view Tolstoy's literary career as divided into two halves, the first half ending with the completion of *Anna Karenina* in 1877. This first period is considered his best, a free and good and highly productive time in which Tolstoy's genius was not encumbered by theories and false notions. The second half, according to this conventional view, was marred by an interest in propaganda, a diminishing of his creative powers, and an increasing retreat from the secular world into religion. This view, however, overlooks the fact that in each period Tolstoy was both productive and concerned about spiritual things. This view also places less value on his religious works, an assessment that history disputes.

I believe a similar mistake has been made regarding his gospel stories. From a Christian perspective, they are arguably as valuable as *War and Peace.* Tolstoy, from the very beginning, was passionately interested in spiritual questions, and, for at least some of the time, he sought spiritual solutions. He was, according to one scholar, curious about humankind's motives and behavior, about "what was just and what unjust, what noble, what evil, what pure, what impure."[3] All his life he had sought answers to these questions, and as he grew older the search intensified.

Tolstoy's nonfiction writings from the second half of his literary career have had an enormous impact on the world. Mahatma Gandhi read Tolstoy's works while he was in South Africa. Gandhi learned the concept of passive resistance from Tolstoy's pacifist writings, and young Gandhi wrote to Tolstoy about the conditions of laborers in South Africa and later about oppressive conditions in India under British rule. Tolstoy greatly encouraged Gandhi in his civil disobedience and passive resistance campaigns. As biographer A. N. Wilson notes,

> For Tolstoy, the struggle was the same, whether it was the people of Russia against their Government, or the peoples of the Transvaal against the English, or the Negro against his American Oppressors. . . . "What are needed for the Indian as for the Englishman, the Frenchman, the German, and the Russian, are not Constitutions and Revolutions, nor all sorts of Conferences and Congresses. . . . Only one thing is needful—the law of love which brings the highest happiness to every individual as well as to all mankind."[4]

Gandhi's nonviolent tactics were used and reused by a wide variety of groups. Martin Luther King Jr. would apply Gandhi's tactics with great success to the American civil rights movement, and they would be used by freedom fighters in Poland, China, South Africa, and countless other places around the world. Tolstoy's influence, through Gandhi and Gandhi's many disciples and imitators, has been huge.

But was Tolstoy a Christian? Tolstoy's nonfiction religious writings are extremely problematic for Christians. These writings contain some of his very finest thoughts and some of his best writing. They also contain what has been called by one historian some of the "silliest nonsense ever written by anyone."[5]

But it is largely through his nonfiction "religious" writings that Western readers first encountered Leo Tolstoy. In 1884 and 1885, English translations of Tolstoy's major religious works were printed in England. These writings were priced cheaply, printed for the most part in tract form, and read by thousands of westerners. The irony is that though Tolstoy is now more widely known throughout the world for his novels, it was his religious writings that first brought him widespread attention in the West.

And there are contradictions and paradoxes in Tolstoy's personal life as well.

Tolstoy's marriage, closely documented in both his and his wife's diaries, was a highly explosive union rife with contention, hostility, and even hatred. Many people who are inspired by Tolstoy's Christian writings are shocked and disillusioned when they learn that the great prophet of peace lived in one of the most miserable marriages in history.

Before he embraced the teachings of Christ, Tolstoy lived the life—especially as a young, single man—of the sensual hedonist, taking his pleasures wherever they were to be found, with whomever struck his fancy. He was a gambler, a womanizer, a drunkard, and an extremist . . . truly a sinner in need of salvation and grace.

The more we come to know about Tolstoy—his numerous contradictions and paradoxes—the less he makes sense. Still, despite his inability to be consistently a good man either within himself or domestically, Tolstoy had a profound sense of morality. He knew what righteousness was. He was in love with goodness and longed to do good deeds.

Around the age of fifty-one, after writing *War and Peace* and *Anna Karenina,* Tolstoy had a personal religious revelation. This followed years of study of the New Testament and of soul-searching for the meaning of life. He began to put his idea of Christianity into practice by trying to serve others as Jesus taught. During the Russian famine of 1891, Tolstoy sponsored 250 relief kitchens in the Moscow slums. He spent ten years (1889 to 1899) writing and serializing a novel, *Resurrection,* which was published internationally in support of the Dukhobors, a peasant religious group that rejected participation in war and practiced a form of Christian communalism.

In 1890, Tolstoy divided his estate among his wife and children and refused to hold any copyrights or property of his own. In an effort to avoid living off the labor of others, he tried to live the life of a peasant. He became a vegetarian, attempted to make his own shoes, and tried to practice celibacy.

Tolstoy's actions caused an international scandal. The celebrated author of *War and Peace* and *Anna Karenina* shocked his admirers by denouncing his own great works as products of an idle brain. Then he continued writing his "religious" nonfiction works and gospel stories such as "Where Love Is, There God Is Also."

But even after he embraced Christianity, Tolstoy's contradictions, paradoxes, and puzzles continued. His ideas, his behavior, and his beliefs were often at odds with the gospel. Tolstoy knew this about himself and made no pretense of being a saint. In his own words:

Well, but you, Lev Nikolayevich; you preach—but how about practice? People always put it to me and always triumphantly shut my mouth with it. You preach, but how do you live? And I reply that I do not preach and cannot preach, though I passionately desire to do so. I could only preach by deeds; and my deeds are bad. What I say is not a sermon but only a refutation of the false understanding of the Christian teaching and an expla-

nation of its real meaning. . . . Blame me—I do that
myself—but blame me and not the path I tread, and show
to those who ask me where in my opinion the road lies!
If I know the road home and go along it drunk, stagger-
ing from side to side—does that make the road along
which I go the wrong one?[6]

There were two strains in Tolstoy's character that are
important for any understanding of his religious views.
One was his skepticism; the other was his exaggerated
capacity to purposefully irritate his reader. These char-
acteristics played themselves out in his life and art in
"bear-baiting exercises" carried to exaggerated extremes.
Tolstoy would—with apparent sincerity and seriousness—
argue the most absurd position, attempting to convince
his listener or reader that apples are purple, or that "bron-
chitis is a metal" rather than an inflammation of the
bronchial tubes. At various times, Tolstoy argued that
Shakespeare was no good, that Jesus was not a Christian,
that Beethoven paled in comparison to folk music, and
that property ownership was a form of high larceny. Tolstoy's quirks undoubtedly influenced his reading of the
Gospels and his concept of Christianity.

Yet, there was in Tolstoy a great desire to make everything clear and simple. In fact, what makes Tolstoy sig-
nificant for our age is his moral directness and simplic-
ity. The New Testament is shrouded in mystery and does
not readily yield itself to clear and simple answers. Nev-

ertheless, what counted most for Tolstoy was the moral and spiritual power of Christ in the lives of men and women. For Tolstoy the most urgent question was, Is the moral teaching of Jesus true? If it is, it makes demands upon us to make changes in our lives.

Tolstoy continued to ask the difficult questions of faith: Should we not actually live as Jesus taught us to live? Should we not expel anger from our hearts, turn the other cheek to those who wrong us, rid ourselves of lust and greed? Was the Sermon on the Mount true? Is not the way of Jesus the only path to life?

Tolstoy believed Christ's words to have absolute moral authority. And Tolstoy shines a spotlight on one of the chinks in the Christian armor—that Christians do not practice what they preach. Even today many Christian believers assert that Jesus was divine and infallible but that there is no need to act on the things he taught. Christians do not want that responsibility to act that the gospel teaches we have. This is the inconsistency that Tolstoy highlights. In his life and in his writings Tolstoy keeps asking the question, How is it that Christians can refuse to obey the words of Christ?

✳ ✳ ✳

The three stories presented in this volume are a testimony to the great gift that God bestowed on Leo Tolstoy. That Tolstoy struggled with doubts and disbelief, that he wrestled often unsuccessfully with his own un-Christ-like nature and natural inclinations, and that he did not always live up to the ideas he advocated does not diminish their power. More Christians should become aware of these stories. And more Christians should become aware of Tolstoy's life as it relates to his beliefs. There is much in the stories and in the life that speaks to us today.

"Where Love Is, There God Is Also," written in 1885, has already been widely used by pulpit storytellers, though few know it by its proper title, and fewer still know that Tolstoy is its author. This tale of the simple shoemaker who believes with childlike faith has few equals in Christian literature depicting the gospel in action.

"The Three Hermits," written in 1886, tells the story of a bishop who learns a very important lesson in holiness from three men living on an otherwise deserted island. These men have dedicated their lives to worshiping God. When the bishop tries to teach them the proper way to pray, he learns that God honors the heart yielded to Him, not mere ritual.

"What Men Live By," written in 1881, is a marvelously evocative tale that seeks to examine the one thing that people really need in order to live. One of God's angels is banished to earth until he has learned three lessons: What is in men, what is not given to men, and what men live by.

We value Tolstoy and find him interesting because of his imagination and what he is able to do with works of the imagination. Many critics have found these gospel stories too preachy and moralizing, their "points" too heavily labored. But as one historian has noted, "[Tolstoy] wrote from conviction. More than anything he had ever desired, he now desired to obey [Christ's] words himself, to identify with the poor and the oppressed, to abandon his wealth, to live in peace and forgiveness with all men. . . . Tolstoy, with . . . imaginative panache, restored to the world Christ's starkest and most revolutionary moral demands."[7]

For the Christian, Tolstoy's gospel stories represent Christ-centered fiction at its best—imaginative narratives that put the gospel message into compelling action.

Lawrence Jordan
New York, New York

Notes

1. A. N. Wilson, *Tolstoy* (New York: W. W. Norton, 1988), 105.

2. Ibid., 249.

3. Charles Neider, ed., *Tolstoy: Tales of Courage and Conflict* (New York: Carroll & Graf, 1985), 15.

4. Wilson, *Tolstoy*, 491.

5. Ibid., 354.

6. Ibid., 397.

7. Ibid., 326.

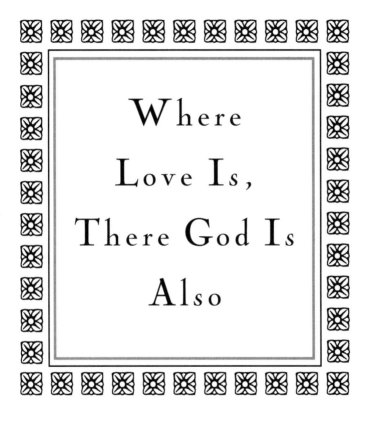

Where
Love Is,
There God Is
Also

n the city lived the shoemaker, Martuin Avdyeitch. He lived in a basement, in a little room with one window. The window looked out on the street. Through the window he used to watch the people passing by; although only their feet could be seen, yet by the boots Martuin Avdyeitch recognized the people. Martuin Avdyeitch had lived long in one place, and had many acquaintances. Few pairs of boots in his district had not been in his hands once and again. Some he would half-sole, some he would patch, some he would stitch around, and occasionally he would also put on new uppers. And through the window he often recognized his work.

Avdyeitch had plenty to do, because he was a faithful workman, used good material, did not make exorbitant charges, and kept his word. If it was possible for him to finish an order by a certain time, he would accept it; otherwise, he would not deceive you—he would tell you so beforehand. And all knew Avdyeitch, and he was never out of work.

Avdyeitch had always been a good man; but as he grew old, he began to think more about his soul, and get nearer to God. Martuin's wife had died when he was still living with his master. His wife left him a boy three years old. None of their other children had lived.

All the eldest had died in childhood. Martuin at first intended to send his little son to his sister in the village, but afterward he felt sorry for him. He thought to himself, *It will be hard for my Kapitoshka to live in a strange family. I shall keep him with me.*

And Avdyeitch left his master, and went into lodgings with his little son. But God gave Avdyeitch no luck with his children. As Kapitoshka grew older, he began to help his father, and would have been a delight to him, but a sickness fell on him, he went to bed, suffered a week, and died. Martuin buried his son, and fell into despair. So deep was this despair that he began to complain of God. Martuin fell into such a melancholy state, that more than once he prayed to God for death, and reproached God because He had not taken him who was an old man, instead of his beloved only son. Avdyeitch also ceased to go to church.

And once a little old man from the same district came from Troitsa ["Trinity," a famous monastery, pilgrimage to which is reckoned a virtue] to see Avdyeitch; for seven years he had been wandering about. Avdyeitch talked with him, and began to complain about his sorrows.

"I have no desire to live any longer," he said. "I only wish I was dead. That is all I pray God for. I am a man without anything to hope for now."

And the little old man said to him, "You don't talk right, Martuin: we must not judge God's doings. The world moves, not by our skill, but by God's will. God decreed for your son to die—for you—to live. So it is for the best. And you are in despair, because you wish to live for your own happiness."

"But what shall one live for?" asked Martuin.

And the little old man said, "We must live for God, Martuin. He gives you life, and for His sake you must live. When you begin to live for Him, you will not grieve over anything, and all will seem easy to you."

Martuin kept silent for a moment, and then said, "But how can one live for God?"

And the little old man said, "Christ has taught us how to live for God. You know how to read? Buy a Testament, and read it; there you will learn how to live for God. Everything is explained there."

And these words kindled a fire in Avdyeitch's heart. And he went that very same day, bought a New Testament in large print, and began to read.

At first Avdyeitch intended to read only on holidays; but as he began to read, it so cheered his soul that he used to read every day. At times he would become so absorbed in reading, that all the kerosene in the lamp would burn out, and still he could not tear himself away. And so Avdyeitch used to read every evening.

And the more he read, the clearer he understood what God wanted of him, and how one should live for God; and his heart kept growing easier and easier. Formerly, when he lay down to sleep, he used to sigh and groan, and always thought of his Kapitoshka; and now his only exclamation was, "Glory to Thee! Glory to Thee, Lord! Thy will be done."

And from that time Avdyeitch's whole life was changed. In other days he, too, used to drop into a public house as a holiday amusement, to drink a cup of tea; and he was not averse to a little brandy either. He would take a drink with some acquaintance, and leave the saloon, not intoxicated exactly, yet in a happy frame of mind, and inclined to talk nonsense, and shout, and use abusive language at a person. Now he left off that sort of thing. His life became quiet and joyful. In the morning he would sit down to work, finish his allotted task, then take the little lamp from the hook, put it on the table, get his book from the shelf, open it, and sit down to read. And the more he read, the more he understood, and the brighter and happier it grew in his heart.

Once it happened that Martuin read till late into the night. He was reading the Gospel of Luke. He was reading over the sixth chapter; and he was reading the verses: "And unto him that smiteth thee on the one cheek offer also the other; and him that taketh away thy cloak, forbid not to take thy coat also. Give to every man that asketh of thee; and of him that taketh away thy goods, ask them not again. And as ye would that men should do to you, do ye also to them likewise."

He read farther also those verses, where God speaks: "And why call ye me, Lord, Lord, and do not the things which I say? Whosoever cometh to me, and heareth my sayings, and doeth them, I will shew you to whom he is like: he is like a man which built an house, and digged deep, and laid the foundation on a rock: and when the flood arose, the stream beat vehemently upon that house, and could not shake it: for it was founded upon a rock. But he that heareth, and doeth not, is like a man that without a foundation built an house upon the earth; against which the stream did beat vehemently, and immediately it fell; and the ruin of that house was great."

Avdyeitch read these words, and joy filled his soul. He took off his spectacles, put them down on the book, leaned his elbows on the table, and became lost in thought. And he began to measure his life by these words. And he thought to himself, *Is my house built on the rock or on the sand? 'Tis well if on the rock. It is so easy when you are alone by yourself; it seems as if you had done everything as God commands; but when you forget yourself, you sin again. Yet I shall still struggle on. It is very good. Help me, Lord!*

Thus ran his thoughts; he wanted to go to bed, but he felt loath to tear himself away from the book. And he began to read farther in the seventh chapter. He read about the centurion, he read about the widow's son, he read about the answer given to John's disciples, and finally he came to that place where the rich Pharisee desired the Lord to sit at meat with him; and he read how the woman that was a sinner anointed His feet, and washed them with her tears, and how He forgave her. He reached the forty-fourth verse, and began to read: "And he turned to the woman, and said unto Simon, Seest thou this woman? I entered into thine house, thou gavest me no water for my feet: but she hath washed my feet with tears, and wiped them with the hairs of her head. Thou gavest me no kiss: but this woman since the time I came in hath not ceased to kiss my feet. My head with oil thou didst not anoint: but this woman hath anointed my feet with ointment."

He finished reading these verses and thought to himself, *Thou gavest me no water for my feet, thou gavest me no kiss. My head with oil thou didst not anoint.*

And again Avdyeitch took off his spectacles, put them down on the book, and again he became lost in thought.

"It seems that Pharisee must have been such a man as I am. I, too, apparently have thought only of myself—how I might have my tea, be warm and comfortable, but never to think about my guest. He thought about himself, but there was not the least care taken of the guest. And who was his guest? The Lord Himself. If He had come to me, should I have done the same way?"

Avdyeitch rested his head upon both his arms, and did not notice that he fell asleep.

"Martuin!" suddenly seemed to sound in his ears.

Martuin started from his sleep. "Who is here?"

He turned around, glanced toward the door—no one.

Again he fell into a doze. Suddenly he plainly heard, "Martuin! Ah, Martuin! Look tomorrow on the street. I am coming."

Martuin awoke, rose from the chair, began to rub his eyes. He himself could not tell whether he heard those words in his dream, or in reality. He turned down his lamp, and went to bed.

At daybreak next morning, Avdyeitch rose, made his prayer to God, lighted the stove, put on the cabbage soup and the gruel, put water in the samovar, put on his apron, and sat down by the window to work.

And while he was working, he kept thinking about all that had happened the day before. It seemed to him at one moment that it was a dream, and now he had really heard a voice.

"Well," he said to himself, "such things have been."

Martuin was sitting by the window and looking out more than he was working. When anyone passed by in boots which he did not know, he would bend down, look out the window, in order to see not only the feet, but also the face.

The house porter passed by in new felt boots, the water carrier passed by; then there came up to the window an old soldier of Nicholas's time, in an old pair of laced felt boots, with a shovel in his hands. Avdyeitch recognized him by his felt boots. The old man's name was Stepanuitch; and a neighboring merchant, out of charity, gave him a home with him. He was required to assist the dvornik. Stepanuitch began to shovel away the snow from in front of Avdyeitch's window. Avdyeitch glanced at him, and took up his work again.

"Pshaw! I must be getting crazy in my old age," said Avdyeitch, and laughed at himself. "Stepanuitch is clearing away the snow, and I imagine that Christ is coming to see me. I was entirely out of my mind, old dotard that I am!"

Avdyeitch sewed about a dozen stitches, and then felt impelled to look through the window again. He looked out again through the window, and saw that Stepanuitch had leaned his shovel against the wall, and was warming himself, and resting. He was an old broken-down man; evidently he had not strength enough even to shovel the snow. Avdyeitch said to himself, "I will give him some tea; by the way, the samovar has only just gone out." Avdyeitch laid down his awl, rose from his seat, put the samovar on the table, poured out the tea, and tapped with his finger at the glass. Stepanuitch turned around, and came to the window. Avdyeitch beckoned to him, and went to open the door.

"Come in, warm yourself a little," he said. "You must be cold."

"May Christ reward you for this! My bones ache," said Stepanuitch.

Stepanuitch came in and shook off the snow, tried to wipe his feet, so as not to soil the floor, but he staggered.

"Don't trouble to wipe your feet. I will clean it up myself; we are used to such things. Come in and sit down," said Avdyeitch. "Here, drink a cup of tea."

And Avdyeitch filled two glasses, and handed one to his guest; while he himself poured his tea into a saucer, and began to blow it.

Stepanuitch finished drinking his glass of tea, turned the glass upside down [to signify he was satisfied, a custom among the Russians], put the half-eaten lump of sugar on it, and began to express his thanks. But it was evident he wanted some more.

"Have some more," said Avdyeitch, filling both his own glass and his guest's. Avdyeitch drank his tea, but from time to time glanced out into the street.

"Are you expecting anyone?" asked his guest.

"Am I expecting anyone? I am ashamed even to tell whom I expect. I am, and I am not, expecting someone; but one word has kindled a fire in my heart. Whether it is a dream, or something else, I do not know. Don't you see, brother, I was reading yesterday the Gospel about Christ the Batyushka; how He suffered, how He walked on the earth. I suppose you have heard about it?"

"Indeed I have," replied Stepanuitch; "but we are people in darkness, we can't read."

"Well, now, I was reading about that very thing—how He walked on the earth; I read, you know, how He came to the Pharisee, and the Pharisee did not treat Him hospitably. Well, and so, my brother, I was reading yesterday, about this very thing, and was thinking to myself how he did not receive Christ the Batyushka, with honor. Suppose, for example, He should come to me, or anyone else, I said to myself, I should not even know how to receive Him. And he gave Him no reception at all. Well! while I was thus thinking, I fell asleep, brother, and I heard someone call me by name. I got up; the voice, just as if someone whispered, said, 'Be on the watch; I shall come tomorrow.' And this happened twice. Well! would you believe it, it got into my head? I scolded myself—and yet I am expecting Him, the Batyushka."

Stepanuitch shook his head, and said nothing; he finished drinking his glass of tea, and put it on the side; but Avdyeitch picked up the glass again, and filled it once more.

"Drink some more for your good health. You see, I have an idea that, when the Batyushka went about on this earth, He disdained no one, and had more to do with the simple people. He always went to see the simple people. He picked out His disciples more from among folk like such sinners as we are, from the working class. Said He, whoever exalts himself, shall be humbled, and he who is humbled shall become exalted. Said He, you call me Lord, and, said He, I wash your feet. Whoever wishes, said He, to be the first, the same shall be a servant to all.

Because, said He, blessed are the poor, the humble, the kind, the generous."

And Stepanuitch forgot about his tea; he was an old man, and easily moved to tears. He was listening, and the tears rolled down his face.

"Come, now, have some more tea," said Avdyeitch; but Stepanuitch made the sign of the cross, thanked him, turned down his glass, and arose.

"Thanks to you," he says, "Martuin Avdyeitch, for treating me kindly, and satisfying me, soul and body."

"You are welcome; come in again; always glad to see a friend," said Avdyeitch.

Stepanuitch departed; and Martuin poured out the rest of the tea, drank it up, put away the dishes, and sat down again by the window to work, to stitch on a patch. He kept stitching away, and at the same time looking through the window. He was expecting Christ, and was all the while thinking of Him and His deeds, and his head was filled with the different speeches of Christ.

Two soldiers passed by: one wore boots furnished by the crown, and the other one, boots that he had made; then the master of the next house passed by in shining galoshes; then a baker with a basket passed by. All passed by; and now there came also by the window a woman in woolen stockings and rustic bashmaks on her feet. She passed by the window, and stood still near the window case.

Avdyeitch looked up at her from the window, and saw it was a stranger, a woman poorly clad, and with a child; she was standing by the wall with her back to the wind, trying to wrap up the child, and she had nothing to wrap it up in. The woman was dressed in shabby summer clothes; from behind the frame, Avdyeitch could hear the child crying, and the woman trying to pacify it; but she was not able to pacify it.

Avdyeitch got up, went to the door, ascended the steps, and cried, "My good woman. Hey! My good woman!"

The woman heard him and turned around.

"Why are you standing in the cold with the child? Come into my room, where it is warm; you can manage it better. Here, this way!"

The woman was astonished. She saw an old, old man, in an apron, with spectacles on his nose, calling her to him. She followed him. They descended the steps and entered the room; the old man led the woman to his bed.

"There," says he. "Sit down, my good woman, nearer to the stove; you can get warm, and nurse the little one."

"I have no milk for him. I myself have not eaten anything since morning," said the woman; but, nevertheless, she took the baby to her breast.

Avdyeitch shook his head, went to the table, brought out the bread and a dish, opened the oven door, poured into the dish some cabbage soup, took out the pot with the gruel, but it was not cooked as yet, so he filled the dish with shchi only, and put it on the table. He got the bread, took the towel down from the hook, and spread it upon the table.

"Sit down," he says, "and eat, my good woman; and I will mind the little one. You see, I once had children of my own; I know how to handle them."

The woman crossed herself, sat down at the table, and began to eat; while Avdyeitch took a seat on the bed near the infant. Avdyeitch kept smacking and smacking to it with his lips; but it was a poor kind of smacking, for he had no teeth. The little one kept on crying. And it occurred to Avdyeitch to threaten the little one with his finger; he waved, waved his finger right before the child's mouth, and hastily withdrew it. He did not put it to its mouth, because his finger was black, and soiled with wax. And the little one looked at his finger, and became quiet; then it began to smile, and Avdyeitch also was glad. While the woman was eating, she told who she was, and whither she was going.

Said she, "I am a soldier's wife. It is now seven months since they sent my husband away off, and no tidings. I lived out as cook; the baby was born; no one cared to keep me with a child. This is the third month that I have been struggling along without a place. I ate all I had. I wanted to engage as a wet nurse—no one would take me—I am too thin, they say. I have just been to the merchant's wife, where lives a young woman I know, and they promised to take us in. I thought that was the end of it. But she told me to come next week. And she lives a long way off. I got tired out; and it tired him too, my heart's darling. Fortunately our landlady takes pity on us for the sake of Christ, and gives us a room, else I don't know how I should manage to get along."

Avdyeitch sighed and said, "Haven't you any warm clothes?"

"Now is the time, friend, to wear warm clothes; but yesterday I pawned my last shawl for a twenty-kopek piece."

The woman came to the bed, and took the child; and Avdyeitch rose, went to the partition, rummaged round, and succeeded in finding an old coat.

"Na!" says he; "it is a poor thing, yet you may turn it to some use."

The woman looked at the coat and looked at the old man; she took the coat, and burst into tears; Avdyeitch turned away his head; crawling under the bed, he pushed out a little trunk, rummaged in it, and sat down again opposite the woman.

And the woman said, "May Christ bless you, little grandfather! He must have sent me to your window. My little baby would have frozen to death. When I started out it was warm, but now it has grown cold. And He, the Batyushka, led you to look through the window and take pity on me, an unfortunate."

Avdyeitch smiled and said, "Indeed, He did that! I have been looking through the window, my good woman, for some wise reason."

And Martuin told the soldier's wife his dream, and how he heard the voice—how the Lord promised to come and see him that day.

"All things are possible," said the woman. She rose, put on the coat, wrapped up her little child in it; and, as she started to take leave, she thanked Avdyeitch again.

"Take this, for Christ's sake," said Avdyeitch, giving her a twenty-kopek piece; "redeem your shawl."

She made the sign of the cross, and Avdyeitch made the sign of the cross and went with her to the door.

The woman went away. Avdyeitch ate some shchi, washed the dishes, and sat down again to work. While he was working he still remembered the window; when the window grew darker he immediately looked out to see who was passing by. Acquaintances passed by and strangers passed by, and there was nothing out of the ordinary.

But here Avdyeitch saw that an old apple-woman had stopped in front of his window. She carried a basket with apples. Only a few were left, as she had evidently sold them nearly all out; and over her shoulder she had a bag full of wood chips. She must have gathered them up in some new building, and was on her way home. One could see that the bag was heavy on her shoulder; she tried to shift it to the other shoulder. So she lowered the bag on the sidewalk, stood the basket with the apples on a little post, and began to shake down the splinters in the bag. And while she was shaking her bag, a little boy in a torn cap came along, picked up an apple from the basket, and was about to make his escape; but the old woman noticed it, turned around, and caught the youngster by his sleeve. The little boy began to struggle, tried to tear himself away; but the old woman grasped him with both hands, knocked off his cap, and caught him by the hair.

The little boy was screaming, the old woman was scolding. Avdyeitch lost no time in putting away his awl; he threw it upon the floor, sprang to the door—he even stumbled on the stairs, and dropped his spectacles—and rushed out into the street.

The old woman was pulling the youngster by his hair, and was scolding, threatening to take him to the policeman; the youngster was defending himself, and denying the charge.

"I did not take it," he said; "what are you licking me for? Let me go!"

Avdyeitch tried to separate them. He took the boy by his arm, and said, "Let him go, babushka; forgive him, for Christ's sake."

"I will forgive him so that he won't forget it till the new broom grows. I am going to take the little villain to the police."

Avdyeitch began to entreat the old woman, "Let him go, babushka," he said. "He will never do it again. Let him go, for Christ's sake."

The old woman let him loose; the boy started to run, but Avdyeitch kept him back.

"Ask the babushka's forgiveness," he said, "and don't you ever do it again; I saw you take the apple."

The boy burst into tears, and began to ask forgiveness.

"There now! that's right; and here's an apple for you."

And Avdyeitch took an apple from the basket, and gave it to the boy.

"I will pay you for it, babushka," he said to the old woman.

"You ruin them that way, the good-for-nothings," said the old woman. "He ought to be treated so that he would remember it for a whole week."

"Eh, babushka, babushka," said Avdyeitch, "that is right according to our judgment, but not according to God's. If he is to be whipped for an apple, then what ought to be done to us for our sins?"

The old woman was silent.

And Avdyeitch told her the parable of the master who forgave a debtor all that he owed him, and how the debtor went and began to choke one who owed him.

The old woman listened, and the boy stood listening.

"God has commanded us to forgive," said Avdyeitch, "else we, too, may not be forgiven. All should be forgiven, and the thoughtless especially."

The old woman shook her head, and sighed. "That's so," said she; "but the trouble is that they are very much spoiled."

"Then, we who are older must teach them," said Avdyeitch.

"That's just what I say," remarked the old woman. "I myself have had seven of them—only one daughter is left."

And the old woman began to relate where and how she lived with her daughter, and how many grandchildren she had. "Here," she says, "my strength is only so-so, and yet I have to work. I pity the youngsters—my grandchildren—but what nice children they are! No one gives me such a welcome as they do. Aksintka won't go to anyone but me. 'Babushka, dear babushka, loveliest.'"

And the old woman grew quite sentimental.

"Of course, it is a childish trick. God be with him," said she, pointing to the boy.

The woman was just about to lift the bag up on her shoulder, when the boy ran up, and said, "Let me carry it, babushka; it is on my way."

The old woman nodded her head and put the bag on the boy's back.

And side by side they passed along the street.

And the old woman even forgot to ask Avdyeitch to pay for the apple. Avdyeitch stood motionless, and kept gazing after them; and he heard them talking all the time as they walked away. After Avdyeitch saw them disappear, he returned to his room; he found his eyeglasses on the stairs—they were not broken; he picked up his awl, and sat down to work again.

After working a little while it grew darker, so that he could not see to sew; he saw the lamplighter passing by to light the streetlamps.

"It must be time to make a light," he said to himself; so he got his little lamp ready, hung it up, and betook himself again to his work. He had one boot already finished; he turned it around, and looked at it: "Well done." He put away his tools, swept off the cuttings, cleared off the bristles and ends, took the lamp, and set it on the table and took down the Gospels from the shelf. He intended to open the book at the very place where he had yesterday put a piece of leather as a mark, but it happened to open at another place; and the moment Avdyeitch opened the Testament, he recollected his last night's dream. And as soon as he remembered it, it seemed as if he heard someone stepping about behind him. Avdyeitch looked around, and saw—there in the dark corner, it seemed as if people were standing; he was at a loss to know who they were. And a voice whispered in his ear, "Martuin—ah, Martuin! Did you not recognize Me?"

"Who?" exclaimed Avdyeitch.

"Me," repeated the voice. "It was I"; and Stepanuitch stepped forth from the dark corner; he smiled and like a little cloud faded away, and soon vanished. . . .

"And it was I," said the voice.

From the dark corner stepped forth the woman with her child; the woman smiled, the child laughed, and they also vanished.

"And it was I," continued the voice; both the old woman and the boy with the apple stepped forward; both smiled and vanished.

Avdyeitch's soul rejoiced; he crossed himself, put on his spectacles, and began to read the Evangelists where it happened to open. On the upper part of the page he read: "For I was an hungered, and ye gave me meat: I was thirsty, and ye gave me drink: I was a stranger, and ye took me in. . . ."

And on the lower part of the page he read this: "Inasmuch as ye have done it unto one of the least of these my brethren, ye have done it unto me" (Matthew 25).

And Avdyeitch understood that his dream had not deceived him; the Savior really called on him that day, and that he really received Him.

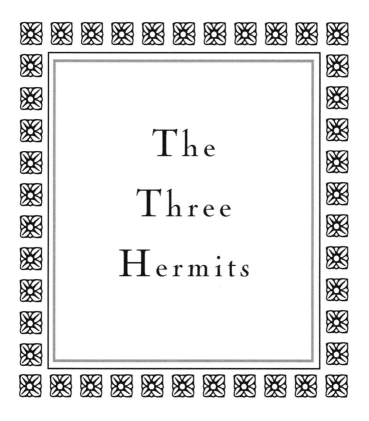

The
Three
Hermits

❋ ❋ ❋

But when ye pray, use not vain repetitions, as the heathen do: for they think that they shall be heard for their much speaking. Be not ye therefore like unto them: for your Father knoweth what things ye have need of, before ye ask him.

Matthew 6:7–8

❋ ❋ ❋

bishop set sail in a ship from the city of Archangelsk to Solovki [the Slovetsky Monastery, at the mouth of the Dvina River]. In the same ship sailed some pilgrims to the saints.

The wind was propitious, the weather was clear, the sea was not rough. The pilgrims, some of whom were lying down, some lunching, some sitting in little groups, conversed together.

The bishop also came on deck and began to walk up and down on the bridge. As he approached the bow, he saw a knot of people crowded together. A little muzhik was pointing his hand at something in the sea, and talking; and the people were listening.

The bishop stood still, and looked where the little muzhik was pointing; nothing was to be seen, except the sea glittering in the sun.

The bishop came closer and began to listen. When the little muzhik saw the bishop, he took off his cap, and stopped speaking. The people also, when they saw the bishop, took off their hats, and paid their respects.

"Don't mind me, brothers," said the bishop. "I have also come to listen to what you are saying, my good friend."

"This fisherman was telling us about some hermits," said a merchant, who was bolder than the rest.

"What about the hermits?" asked the bishop, as he came to the gunwale, and sat down on a box. "Tell me too; I should like to hear. What were you pointing at?"

"Well, then, yonder's the little island just heaving in sight," said the little peasant; and he pointed toward the port side. "On that very islet, three hermits live, working out their salvation."

"Where is the little island?" asked the bishop.

"Here, look along my arm, if you please. You see that little cloud? Well, just below it to the left it shows like a streak."

The bishop looked and looked; the water gleamed in the sun, but from lack of practice he could not see anything.

"I don't see it," says he. "What sort of hermits are they who live on the little island?"

"God's people," replied the peasant. "For a long time I had heard tell of them, but I never chanced to see them until last summer."

And the fisherman again began to relate how he had been out fishing, and how he was driven to that island, and knew not where he was. In the morning he started to look around, and stumbled upon a little earthen hut; and he found in the hut one hermit, and then two others came in. They fed him, and dried him, and helped him repair his boat.

"What sort of men were they?" asked the bishop.

"One was rather small, humpbacked, very, very old; he was dressed in a well-worn stole; he must have been more than a hundred years old; the gray hairs in his beard were already turning green; but he always had a smile ready, and he was as serene as an angel of heaven. The second was taller, also old, in a torn kaftan; his long beard was growing a little yellowish, but he was a strong man; he turned my boat over as if it had been a tub, and I didn't even have to help him: he was also a jolly man. But the third was tall, with a long beard reaching to his knee, and white as the moon; but he was gloomy; his eyes glared out from under beetling brows; and he was all naked, all save a plaited belt."

"What did they say to you?" asked the bishop.

"They did everything mostly without speaking, and they talked very little among themselves; one had only to look, and the other understood. I began to ask the tall one if they had lived here long. He frowned, muttered something, grew almost angry: then the little old man instantly seized him by the hand, smiled, and the large man said nothing. But the old man said, 'Excuse us,' and smiled."

While the peasant was speaking, the ship had been sailing nearer and nearer to the islands.

"There, now you can see plainly," said the merchant. "Now please look, your reverence," said he, pointing.

The bishop tried to look, and he barely managed to make out a black speck—the little island.

The bishop gazed and gazed; and he went from the bow to the stern, and he approached the helmsman.

"What is that little island," says he, "that you see over yonder?"

"As far as I know, it has no name; there are a good many of them here."

"Is it true as they say, that some monks are winning their salvation there?"

"They say so, your reverence, but I don't rightly know. Fishermen, they say, have seen them. Still, folks talk a good deal of nonsense."

"I should like to land on the little island, and see the hermits," said the bishop. "How can I manage it?"

"It is impossible to go there in the ship," said the helmsman. "You might do it in a boat, but you will have to ask the captain."

They summoned the captain.

"I should like to have a sight of those hermits," said the bishop. "Is it out of the question to take me there?"

The captain tried to dissuade him.

"It is possible, quite possible, but we should waste much time; and I take the liberty of assuring your reverence, they are not worth looking at. I have heard from people that those old men are perfectly stupid; they don't understand anything, and can't say anything, just like some sort of sea-fish."

"I wish it," said the bishop. "I will pay for the trouble, if you will take me there."

There was nothing else to be done: the sailors arranged it; they shifted sail. The helmsman put the ship about and they sailed toward the island. A chair was set for the bishop on the bow. He sat down and looked. And all the people gathered on the bow, all looked at the little island. And those who had trustworthy eyes already began to see rocks on the island, and point out the hut. And one even saw the three hermits. The captain got out a spyglass, gazed through it, handed it to the bishop.

"He is quite right," said the captain; "there on the shore at the right, standing on a great rock, are three men."

The bishop also looked through the glass; he pointed it in the right direction and plainly saw the three men standing there—one tall, the second shorter, but the third very short. They were standing on the shore, hand in hand.

The captain came to the bishop, "Here, your reverence, the ship must come to anchor; if it suit you, you can be put ashore in a yawl, and we will anchor out here and wait for you."

Immediately they got the tackle ready, cast anchor, and furled the sails; the vessel brought up, began to roll. They lowered a boat, the rowers manned it, and the bishop started to climb down by the companionway. The bishop climbed down, took his seat on the thwart; the rowers lifted their oars; they sped away to the island. They sped away like a stone from a sling; they could see the three men standing—the tall one naked, with his plaited belt; the shorter one in his torn kaftan; and the little old humpbacked one, in his old stole—all three were standing there, hand in hand.

The sailors reached shore and caught hold with the boat-hook. The bishop got out.

The hermits bowed before him; he blessed them; they bowed still lower. And the bishop began to speak to them.

"I heard," says he, "that you hermits were here, working out your salvation, that you pray Christ our God for your fellowmen; and I am here by God's grace, an unworthy servant of Christ, called to be a shepherd to His flock; and so I desired also, if I might, to give instructions to you, who are the servants of God."

The hermits made no reply; they smiled, they exchanged glances.

"Tell me how you are working out your salvation, and how you serve God," said the bishop.

The middle hermit sighed, and looked at the aged one, at the venerable one; the tall hermit frowned, and looked at the aged one, at the venerable one. And the venerable old hermit smiled, and said, "Servant of God, we have not the skill to serve God; we serve only ourselves, getting something to eat."

"How do you pray to God?" asked the bishop.

And the venerable hermit said, "We pray thus: 'You three, have mercy on us three.'"

And as soon as the venerable hermit said this, all three of the hermits raised their eyes to heaven, and all three said, *"Troe vas, troe nas, pomiluï nas!"*

The bishop smiled, and said, "You have heard this about the Holy Trinity, but you should not pray so. I have taken a fancy to you, men of God. I see that you desire to please God, but you know not how to serve Him. You should not pray so; but listen to me, I will teach you from God's Scriptures how God commanded all people to pray to God."

And the bishop began to explain to the hermits how God revealed Himself to men. He taught them about God the Father, God the Son, and God the Holy Spirit, and said, "God the Son come to earth to save men, and this is the way He taught all men to pray; listen, and repeat after me:

And the bishop began to say, *"Our Father."*

And one hermit repeated, *"Our Father."*

And the second repeated, *"Our Father."*

And the third also repeated, *"Our Father."*

"Who art in heaven;" and the hermits tried to repeat, *"Who art in heaven."*

But the middle hermit mixed the words up, he could not repeat them so; and the tall, naked hermit could not repeat them—his mustache had grown so as to cover his mouth, he could not speak distinctly; and the venerable, toothless hermit could not stammer the words intelligibly.

The bishop said it a second time; the hermits repeated it again. And the bishop sat down on a little boulder, and the hermits stood about him; and they looked at his lips, and they repeated it after him until they knew it. And all that day till evening the bishop labored with them; and ten times, and twenty times, and a hundred times, he repeated each word, and the hermits learned it by rote. And when they got mixed up, he set them right, and made them begin all over again.

And the bishop did not leave the hermits until he had taught them the whole of the Lord's Prayer. They repeated it after him, and then by themselves.

First of all, the middle hermit learned it, and he repeated it from beginning to end; and the bishop bade him say it again and again, and still again to repeat it; and the others also learned the whole prayer.

It was already beginning to grow dark, and the moon was just coming up out of the sea, when the bishop arose to go back to the ship.

The bishop said farewell to the hermits; they all bowed very low before him. He raised them to their feet and kissed each of them, bade them pray as he had taught them; and he took his seat in the boat, and returned to the ship.

And while the bishop was rowed back to the ship, he heard all the time how the hermits were repeating the Lord's Prayer at the top of their voices.

They returned to the ship, and here the voices of the hermits could no longer be heard; but they could still see, in the light of the moon, the three old men standing in the very same place on the shore—one shorter than the rest in the middle, with the tall one on the right, and the other one on the left hand.

The bishop returned to the ship, climbed up on deck; the anchor was hoisted; the sails were spread, and bellied with the wind; the ship began to move, and they sailed away.

The bishop came to the stern, and took a seat there, and kept looking at the little island. At first the hermits were to be seen; then they were hidden from sight, and only the island was visible; and then the island went out of sight, and only the sea was left playing in the moonlight.

The pilgrims lay down to sleep, and all was quiet on deck. But the bishop cared not to sleep; he sat by himself in the stern, looked out over the sea in the direction where the island had faded from sight, and thought about the good hermits.

He thought of how they had rejoiced in what they had learned in the prayer; and he thanked God because He had led him to the help of the hermits, in teaching them the Word of God.

Thus the bishop was sitting and thinking, looking at the sea in the direction where the little island lay hidden. And his eyes were filled with the moonlight, as it danced here and there on the waves. Suddenly he saw something shining and gleaming white in the track of the moon. Was it a bird, a gull, or a boat-sail gleaming white? The bishop strained his sight.

A sailboat, he said to himself, *is chasing us. Yes, it is catching up with us very rapidly. It was far, far off, but now it is close to us. But, after all, it is not much like a sailboat. Anyway, something is chasing us and catching up with us.*

And the bishop could not decide what it was—a boat, or not a boat; a bird, or not a bird; a fish, or not a fish. It was like a man, but very great; but a man could not be in the midst of the sea.

The bishop got up and went to the helmsman.

"Look!" says he, "what is that? what is that, brother? what is it?" said the bishop.

But by this time he himself saw. It was the hermits running over sea. Their gray beards gleamed white, and shone; and they drew near the ship as if it were stationary.

The helmsman looked. He was scared, dropped the tiller, and cried with a loud voice, "Lord! the hermits are running over the sea as if it were dry land!"

The people heard and sprang up; all rushed aft. All beheld the hermits running, hand in hand. The end ones swung their arms; they signaled the ship to come to. All three ran over the water as if it were dry land, and did not move their feet.

It was not possible to bring the ship to before the hermits overtook it, came on board, raised their heads, and said with one voice, "We have forgotten, servant of God, we have forgotten what thou didst teach us. While we were learning it, we remembered it; but when we ceased for an hour to repeat it, one word slipped away; we have forgotten it; the whole was lost. We remembered none of it; teach it to us again."

The bishop crossed himself, bowed low to the hermits, and said, "Acceptable to God is your prayer, ye hermits. It is not for me to teach you. Pray for us sinners."

And the bishop bowed before the feet of the hermits. And the hermits paused, turned about, and went back over the sea. And until morning, there was something seen shining in the direction where the hermits had gone.

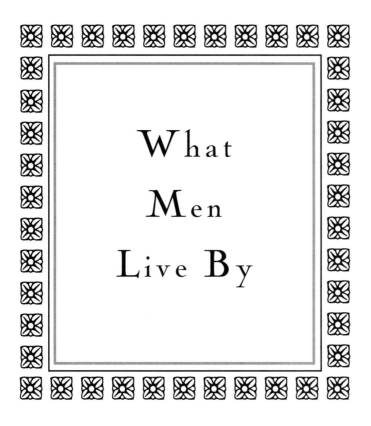

What
Men
Live By

❋ ❋ ❋

We know that we have passed from death unto life, because we love the brethren. He that loveth not his brother abideth in death.

1 John 3:14

But whoso hath this world's good, and seeth his brother have need, and shutteth up his bowels of compassion from him, how dwelleth the love of God in him? My little children, let us not love in word, neither in tongue; but in deed and in truth.

3:17–18

Love is of God; and every one that loveth is born of God, and knoweth God. He that loveth not knoweth not God; for God is love.

4:7–8

No man hath seen God at any time. If we love one another, God dwelleth in us.

4:12

God is love; and he that dwelleth in love dwelleth in God, and God in him.

4:16

If a man say, I love God, and hateth his brother, he is a liar: for he that loveth not his brother whom he hath seen, how can he love God whom he hath not seen?

4:20

❋ ❋ ❋

cobbler and his wife and children had lodgings with a peasant. He owned neither house nor land, and he supported himself and his family by shoemaking.

Bread was dear and labor was poorly paid, and whatever he earned went for food.

The cobbler and his wife had one shuba [fur or sheepskin outer garment] between them, and this had come to tatters, and for two years the cobbler had been hoarding in order to buy sheepskins for a new shuba.

When autumn came, the cobbler's hoard had grown; three paper rubles lay in his wife's box, and five rubles and twenty kopeks more were due the cobbler from his customers.

One morning the cobbler betook himself to the village to get his new shuba. He put on his wife's wadded rankeen jacket over his shirt, and outside of all a woolen kaftan. He put the three-ruble note in his pocket, broke off a staff, and after breakfast he set forth.

He said to himself, *I will get my five rubles from the peasant, and that with these will buy pelts for my shuba.*

The cobbler reached the village and went to one peasant's; he was not at home, but his wife promised to send her husband with the money the next week, but she could not give him any money. He went to another, and this peasant swore that he had no money at all; but he paid him twenty kopeks for cobbling his boots.

The cobbler made up his mind to get the pelts on credit. But the fur-dealer refused to sell on credit.

"Bring the money," said he; "then you can make your choice, but we know how hard it is to get what is one's due."

And so the cobbler did not do his errand, but he had the twenty kopeks for cobbling the boots, and he took from a peasant an old felt pair of boots to mend with leather.

At first the cobbler was vexed at heart; then he spent the twenty kopeks for vodka, and started to go home. In the morning he had felt cold, but after having drunk the brandy he was warm enough even without the shuba.

The cobbler was walking along the road, striking frozen ground with the staff which he had in one hand, and swinging the felt boots in the other, and thus he talked to himself.

I am warm even without a shuba, said he. *I drank a glass, and it dances through all my veins. And so I don't need a sheep-skin coat. I walk along, and all my vexation is forgotten. What a fine fellow I am! What do I need? I can get along without the shuba. I don't need it at all. There's one thing: the wife will feel bad. Indeed, it is too bad; here I have been working for it, and now to have missed it! You just wait now! if you don't bring the money I will take your hat, I vow I will! What a way of doing things! He pays me twenty kopeks at a time! Now what can you do with twenty kopeks? Get a drink; that's all! You say, "I am poor!" But if you are poor, how is it with me? You have a house and cattle and everything; I have nothing but my own hands. You raise your own grain, but I have to buy mine, when I can, and it costs me three rubles a week for food alone. When I get home now, we shall be out of bread. Another ruble and a half of outgo! So you must give me what you owe me.*

By this time the cobbler had reached the chapel at the crossroads, and he saw something white behind the chapel.

It was already twilight, and the cobbler strained his eyes, but he could not make out what the object was.

There never was any such stone there, he said to himself. *A cow? But it does not look like a cow! The head is like a man's; but what is that white? And why should there by any man there?*

He went nearer. Now he could see plainly. What a strange thing! It was indeed a man, but was he alive or dead? sitting there stark naked, leaning against the chapel, and not moving.

The cobbler was frightened. He said to himself, *Someone has killed that man, stripped him, and flung him down there. If I go near, I may get into trouble.*

And the cobbler hurried by.

In passing the chapel he could no longer see the man; but after he was fairly beyond it, he looked back, and saw that the man was no longer leaning against the chapel, but was moving, and apparently looking after him.

The cobbler was still more scared by this, and he said to himself, *Shall I go back to him or go on? If I go back to him, there might be something unpleasant happen; who knows what sort of a man he is? He can't have gone there for any good purpose. If I went to him, he might spring on me and choke me, and I could not get away from him; and even if he did not choke me, why should I try to make his acquaintance? What could be done with him, naked as he is? I can't take him with me, and give him my own clothes! That would be absurd.*

And the cobbler hastened his steps. He had already gone some distance beyond the chapel, when his conscience began to prick him.

He stopped short.

What is this that you are doing, Semyon? he asked himself. *A man is perishing of cold, and you are frightened, and hurry by! Are you so very rich? Are you afraid of losing your money? Aï, Sema! That is not right!*

Semyon turned and went back to the man.

❋ ❋ ❋

Semyon went back to the man, looked at him, and saw that it was a young man in the prime of life; there were no bruises visible on him, but he was evidently freezing and afraid; he was sitting there, leaning back, and he did not look at Semyon; apparently he was so weak he could not lift his eyes.

Semyon went up close to him, and suddenly the man seemed to revive; he lifted his head and fastened his eyes on Semyon.

And by this glance the man won Semyon's heart.

He threw the felt boots down on the ground, took off his belt, and laid it on the boots, and pulled off his kaftan.

"There's nothing to be said," he exclaimed. "Put these on! There now!"

Semyon put his hand under the man's elbow, to help him, and tried to lift him. The man got up.

And Semyon saw that his body was graceful and clean, that his hands and feet were comely, and that his face was agreeable. Semyon threw the kaftan over his shoulders. He could not get his arms into the sleeves. Semyon found the place for him, pulled the coat up, wrapped it around him, and fastened the belt.

He took off his tattered cap, and was going to give it to the stranger, but his head felt cold, and he said to himself, *The whole top of my head is bald, but he has long curly hair.*

So he put his hat on again.

I had better let him put on my boots.

He made him sit down and put the felt boots on him.

After the cobbler had thus dressed him, he says: "There now, brother, just stir about, and you will get warmed up. All these things are in other hands than ours. Can you walk?"

The man stood up, looked affectionately at Semyon, but was unable to speak a word.

"Why don't you say something? We can't spend the winter here. We must get to shelter. Now, then, lean on my stick, if you don't feel strong enough. Bestir yourself!"

And the man started to move. And he walked easily, and did not lag behind. As they walked along the road Semyon said, "Where are you from, if I may ask?"

"I do not belong hereabouts."

"No; I know all the people of this region. How did you happen to come here and get to that chapel?"

"I cannot tell you."

"Someone must have treated you outrageously."

"No one has treated me outrageously. God has punished me."

"God does all things, but you must have been on the road bound for somewhere. Where do you want to go?"

"It makes no difference to me."

Semyon was surprised. The man did not look like a malefactor, and his speech was gentle, but he seemed reticent about himself.

And Semyon said to himself, *Such things as this do not happen every day.* And he said to the man, "Well, come to my house, though you will find it very narrow quarters."

As Semyon approached the yard, the stranger did not lag behind, but walked abreast of him. The wind had arisen, and searched under Semyon's shirt, and as the effect of the wine had now passed away, he began to be chilled to the bone. He walked along, and began to snuffle, and he muffled his wife's jacket closer around him, and he said to himself, *That's the way you get a shuba! You go after a shuba, and you come home without your kaftan! yes, and you bring with you a naked man—besides, Matriona won't take kindly to it!*

And as soon as the thought of Matriona occurred to him, he began to feel downhearted.

But as soon as his eyes fell on the stranger, he remembered what a look he had given him behind the chapel, and his heart danced with joy.

※ ※ ※

Semyon's wife had finished her work early. She had chopped wood, brought water, fed the children, taken her own supper, and was now deliberating when it would be best to mix some bread, *today or tomorrow?*

A large crust was still left. She said to herself, *If Semyon gets something to eat in town, he won't care for much supper, and the bread will last till tomorrow.*

Matriona contemplated the crust for some time, and said, "I am not going to mix any bread. There's just enough flour to make one more loaf. We shall get along till Friday."

Matriona put away the bread, and sat down at the table to sew a patch on her husband's shirt.

She sewed, and thought how her husband would be buying sheepskins for the shuba.

I hope the fur-dealer will not cheat him. For he is as simple as he can be. He, himself, would not cheat anybody, but a baby could lead him by the nose. Eight rubles is no small sum. You can get a fine shuba with it. Perhaps not one tanned, but still a good one. How we suffered last winter without any shuba! Could not go to the river nor anywhere! And whenever he went outdoors, he put on all the clothes, and I hadn't anything to wear. He is late in getting home. He ought to be here by this time. Can my sweetheart have got drunk?

Just as these thoughts were passing through her mind the doorsteps creaked: Someone was at the door. Matriona stuck in the needle, and went to the entry. There she saw the two men had come in—Semyon, and with him a strange peasant, without a cap and in felt boots.

Matriona perceived immediately that her husband's breath smelt of liquor.

Now, she said to herself, *he has gone and got drunk.*

And when she saw that he had not his kaftan on, and wore only her jacket, and had nothing in his hands, and said nothing, but only simpered, Matriona's heart failed within her.

He has drunk up the money, he has been on a spree with this miserable beggar; and, worse than all, he has gone and brought him home!

Matriona let them pass by her into the cottage; then she herself went in; she saw that the stranger was young, and that he had on their kaftan. There was no shift to be seen under the kaftan; and he wore no cap.

As soon as he went in, he paused, and did not move and did not raise his eyes.

And Matriona thought, *He is not a good man; his conscience troubles him.*

Matriona scowled, went to the oven, and watched to see what they would do.

Semyon took off his cap and sat down on the bench good-naturedly.

"Well," said he, "Matriona, can't you get us something to eat?"

Matriona muttered something under her breath.

She did not offer to move, but as she stood by the oven she looked from one to the other and kept shaking her head.

Semyon saw that his wife was out of sorts and would not do anything, but he pretended not to notice it, and took the stranger by the arm.

"Sit down, brother," says he; "we'll have some supper."

The stranger sat down on the bench.

"Well," says Semyon, "haven't you cooked anything?"

Matriona's anger blazed out.

"I cooked," said she, "but not for you. You are a fine man! I see you have been drinking! You went to get a shuba, and you have come home without your kaftan. And, then, you have brought home this naked vagabond with you. I haven't any supper for such drunkards as you are!"

"That'll do, Matriona; what is the use of letting your tongue run on so? If you had only asked first: 'What kind of man . . .'"

"You just tell me what you have done with the money!"

Semyon went to his kaftan, took out the bill, and spread it out.

"Here's the money, but Trifonof did not pay me; he promised it tomorrow."

Matriona grew still more angry.

"You didn't buy the new shuba, and you have given away your only kaftan to this naked vagabond whom you have brought home!"

She snatched the money from the table, and went off to hide it away, saying, "I haven't any supper. I can't feed all your drunken beggars!"

"Hey there! Matriona, just hold your tongue! First you listen to what I have to say . . ."

"Much sense should I hear from a drunken fool! Good reason I had for not wanting to marry such a drunkard as you are. Mother gave me linen, and you have wasted it in drink; you went to get a shuba, and you spent it for drink."

Semyon was going to assure his wife that he had spent only twenty kopeks for drink; he was going to tell her where he had found the man; but Matriona would not give him a chance to speak a word; it was perfectly marvelous, but she managed to speak two words at once! Things that had taken place ten years before—she called them all up.

Matriona scolded and scolded; then she sprang at Semyon, and seized him by the sleeve.

"Give me back my jacket! It's the only one I have, and you took it from me and put it on yourself. Give it here, you miserable dog! Bestir yourself, you villain!"

Semyon began to strip off the jacket. As he was pulling his arms out of the sleeves, his wife gave it a twitch and split the jacket up the seams. Matriona snatched the garment away, threw it over her head, and started for the door. She intended to go out, but she paused, and her heart was pulled in two directions—she wanted to vent her spite, and she wanted to find out what kind of man the stranger was.

❋ ❋ ❋

Matriona paused and said, "If he were a good man, then he would not have been naked; why, even now, he hasn't any shirt on; if he had been engaged in decent business, you would have told where you discovered such an elegant fellow!"

"Well, I was going to tell you. I was walking along, and there, behind the chapel, this man was sitting, stark naked, and half frozen to death. It is not summer, mind you, for a naked man! God brought me to him, else he would have perished. Now what could I do? Such things don't happen every day. I took and dressed him, and brought him home with me. Calm your anger. It's a sin, Matriona; we all must die."

Matriona was about to make a surly reply, but her eyes fell on the stranger, and she held her peace.

The stranger was sitting motionless on the edge of the bench, just as he had sat down. His hands were folded on his knees, his head was bent on his breast, his eyes were shut, and he kept frowning, as if something stifled him.

Matriona made no reply.

Semyon went on to say, "Matriona, can it be that God is not in you?"

Matriona heard his words, and glanced again at the stranger, and suddenly her anger vanished. She turned from the door, went to the corner where the oven was, and brought the supper.

She set a bowl on the table, poured out the kvas [fermented drink made of rye meal or soaked bread crumbs], and put on the last of the crust. She gave them the knife and the spoons.

"Have some victuals," she said.

Semyon touched the stranger.

"Draw up, young man," said he.

Semyon cut the bread and crumbled it into the bowl, and they began to eat their supper. And Matriona sat at the end of the table, leaned on her hand, and gazed at the stranger. And Matriona began to feel sorry for him, and she took a fancy to him.

And suddenly the stranger brightened up, ceased to frown, lifted his eyes to Matriona, and smiled.

After they had finished their supper, the woman cleared off the things, and began to question the stranger.

"Where are you from?"

"I do not belong hereabouts."

"How did you happen to get into this road?"

"I cannot tell you."

"Who maltreated you?"

"God punished me."

"And you were lying there stripped?"

"Yes; there I was lying all naked, freezing to death, when Semyon saw me, had compassion on me, took off his kaftan, put it on me, and bade me come home with him. And here you have fed me, given me something to eat and to drink, and have taken pity on me. May the Lord requite you!"

Matriona got up, took from the window Semyon's old shirt which she had been patching, and gave it to the stranger; then she found a pair of drawers and gave them also to him.

"There now," said she, "I see that you have no shirt. Put these things on, and then lie down wherever you please, in the loft or on the oven."

The stranger took off the kaftan, put on the shirt, and went to bed in the loft. Matriona put out the light, took the kaftan, and lay down beside her husband.

Matriona covered herself up with the skirt of the kaftan, but she lay without sleeping; she could not get the thought of the stranger out of her mind.

When she remembered that he had eaten her last crust, and that there was no bread for the morrow, when she remembered that she had given him the shirt and the drawers, she felt disturbed; but then came the thought of how he had smiled at her, and her heart leaped within her.

Matriona lay a long time without falling asleep, and when she heard that Semyon was also awake, she pulled up the kaftan and said, "Semyon!"

"Ha?"

"You ate up the last of the bread, and I did not mix any more. I don't know how we shall get along tomorrow. Perhaps I might borrow some of neighbor Malanya."

"We shall get along; we shall have enough."

The wife lay without speaking. Then she said, "Well, he seems like a good man; but why doesn't he tell us about himself?"

"It must be because he can't."

"Siom!" [diminutive of Semyon, or Simon]

"Ha?"

"We are always giving; why doesn't someone give to us?"

Semyon did not know what reply to make. He said, "You have talked enough!"

Then he turned over and went to sleep.

In the morning Semyon woke up.

❋ ❋ ❋

His children were still asleep; his wife had gone to a neighbor's to get some bread. The stranger of the evening before, dressed in the old shirt and drawers, was sitting alone on the bench, looking up. And his face was brighter than it had been the evening before. And Semyon said, "Well, my dear, the belly asks for bread, and the naked body for clothes. You must earn your own living. What do you know how to do?"

"There is nothing I know how to do."

Semyon was amazed, and he said, "If one has only the mind to, men can learn anything."

"Men work, and I will work."

"What is your name?"

"Mikhaïla."

"Well, Mikhaïla, if you aren't willing to tell about yourself, that is your affair; but you must earn your own living. If you will work as I shall show you, I will keep you."

"The Lord requite you! I am willing to learn; only show me what to do."

Semyon took a thread, drew it through his fingers, and showed him how to make a waxed end.

"It does not take much skill . . . look . . ."

Mikhaïla looked, and then he also twisted the thread between his fingers; he instantly imitated him, and finished the point. Semyon showed him how to make the welt. This also Mikhaïla immediately understood. The shoemaker likewise showed him how to twist the bristle into the thread, and how to use the awl; and these things also Mikhaïla immediately learned to do.

Whatever part of the work Semyon showed him he imitated him in, and in two days he was able to work as if he had been all his life a cobbler. He worked without relaxation, he ate little, and when his work was done he would sit silent, looking up. He did not go on the street, he spoke no more than was absolutely necessary, he never jested, he never laughed.

The only time that he was seen to smile was on the first evening, when the woman got him his supper.

❋ ❋ ❋

Day after day, week after week, rolled by for a whole year.

Mikhaïla lived on in the same way, working for Semyon. And the fame of Semyon's apprentice went abroad; no one, it was said, could make such neat, strong boots as Semyon's apprentice, Mikhaïla. And from all around people came to Semyon to have boots made, and Semyon began to lay up money.

One winter's day, as Semyon and Mikhaïla were sitting at their work, a sleigh drawn by a troïka drove up to the cottage, with a jingling of bells.

They looked out of the window; the sleigh stopped in front of the cottage; a footman jumped down from the box and opened the door. A barin [the ordinary title of any landowner or noble] in a fur coat got out of the sleigh, walked up to Semyon's cottage, and mounted the steps. Matriona hurried to throw the door wide open.

The barin bent his head and entered the cottage; when he drew himself up to his full height, his head almost touched the ceiling; he seemed to take up nearly all the room.

Semyon rose and bowed; he was surprised to see the barin. He had never before seen such a man.

Semyon himself was thin, the stranger was spare, and Matriona was like a dry chip; but this man seemed to be from a different world. His face was ruddy and full, his neck was like a bull's; it seemed as if he were made out of cast iron.

The barin got his breath, took off his shuba, sat down on the bench, and said, "Which is the master shoemaker?"

Semyon stepped out, saying, "I, your honor."

The barin shouted to his footman, "Hey, Fedka [diminutive of Feodor, Theodore], bring me the leather."

The young fellow ran out and brought back a parcel. The barin took the parcel and laid it on the table.

"Open it," said he.

The footman opened it.

The barin touched the leather with his finger, and said to Semyon, "Now listen, shoemaker. Do you see this leather?"

"I see it, your honor," says he.

"Well, do you appreciate what kind of leather it is?"

Semyon felt of the leather, and said, "That's good leather."

"Indeed it's good! Fool that you are! You never in your life saw such before! German leather. It cost twenty rubles."

Semyon was startled. He said, "Where, indeed, could we have seen anything like it?"

"Well, that's all right. Can you make from this leather a pair of boots that will fit me?"

"I can, your honor."

The barin shouted at him, "'Can' is a good word. Now just realize whom you are making these boots for, and out of what kind of leather. You must make a pair of boots, so that when the year is gone they won't have got out of shape, or ripped. If you can, then take the job and cut the leather; but if you can't, then don't take it and don't cut the leather. I will tell you beforehand, if the boots rip or wear out of shape before the year is out, I will have you locked up; but if they don't rip or get out of shape before the end of the year, then I will give you ten rubles for your work."

Semyon was frightened, and was at a loss what to say. He glanced at Mikhaïla. He nudged him with his elbow, and whispered, "Had I better take it?"

Mikhaïla nodded his head, meaning, "You had better take the job."

Semyon took Mikhaïla's advice; he agreed to make a pair of boots that would not rip or wear out of shape before the year was over.

The barin shouted to his footman, ordered him to take the boot from his left foot, then he stretched out his leg.

"Take the measure!"

Semyon cut off a piece of paper seventeen inches long, smoothed it out, knelt down, wiped his hands nicely on his apron, so as not to soil the barin's stockings, and began to take the measure.

Semyon took the measure of the sole, he took the measure of the instep; then he started to measure the calf of the leg, but the paper was not long enough. The leg at the calf was thick as a beam.

"Look out; don't make it too tight around the calf!"

Semyon was going to cut another piece of paper. The barin sat there, rubbing his toes together in his stockings, and looking at the inmates of the cottage; he caught sight of Mikhaïla.

"Who is that yonder?" he asked; "does he belong to you?"

"He is a master workman. He will make the boots."

"Look here," says the barin to Mikhaïla, "remember that they are to be made so as to last a whole year."

Semyon also looked at Mikhaïla; he saw that Mikhaïla was paying no attention, but was standing in the corner, as if he saw someone there behind the barin. Mikhaïla gazed and gazed, and suddenly smiled, and his whole face lighted up.

"What a fool you are, showing your teeth that way! You had better see to it that the boots are ready in time."

And Mikhaïla replied, "They will be ready as soon as they are needed."

"Very well."

The barin drew on his boot, wrapped his shuba round him, and went to the door. But he forgot to stoop, and so struck his head against the lintel.

The barin stormed and rubbed his head; then he got into his sleigh and drove off. After the barin was gone Semyon said, "Well, he's as solid as a rock! You could not kill him with a mallet. His head almost broke the doorpost, but it did not seem to hurt him much."

And Matriona said, "How can they help getting fat, living as they do? Even death does not carry off such a nail as he is."

※ ※ ※

And Semyon said to Mikhaïla, "Now, you see, we have taken this work, and we must do it as well as we can. The leather is expensive, and the barin gruff. We must not make any blunder. Now, your eye has become quicker, and your hand is more skillful than mine; there's the measure. Cut out the leather, and I will be finishing up those vamps."

Mikhaïla did not fail to do as he was told; he took the barin's leather, stretched it out on the table, doubled it over, took the knife, and began to cut.

Matriona came and watched Mikhaïla as he cut, and she was amazed to see what he was doing. For she was used to cobbler's work, and she looked and saw that Mikhaïla was not cutting the leather for boots, but in rounded fashion.

Matriona wanted to speak, but she thought in her own mind, *Of course I can't be expected to understand how to make boots for gentlemen; Mikhaïla must understand it better than I do; I will not interfere.*

After he had cut out the work, he took his waxed ends and began to sew, not as one does in making boots, with double threads, but with one thread, just as slippers are made.

Matriona wondered at this also, but she still did not like to interfere. And Mikhaïla kept on steadily with his work.

It came time for the nooning; Semyon got up, looked, and saw that Mikhaïla had been making slippers out of the barin's leather. Semyon groaned.

How is this? he asked himself. *Mikhaïla has lived with me a whole year, and never made a mistake, and now he has made such a blunder! The barin ordered thick-soled boots, and he has been making slippers without soles! He has ruined the leather. How can I make it right with the barin? We can't find such leather.*

And he said to Mikhaïla, "What is this you have been doing? . . . My dear fellow, you have ruined me! You know the barin ordered boots, and what have you made?"

He was in the midst of his talk with Mikhaïla when a knock came at the rapper; someone was at the door. They looked out of the window, someone had come on horseback, and was fastening the horse. They opened the door. The same barin's footman came walking in.

"Good-day."

"Good-day to you; what is it?"

"My mistress sent me in regard to a pair of boots."

"What about the boots?"

"It is this. My barin does not need the boots; he has gone from this world."

"What is that you say?"

"He did not live to get home from your house; he died in the sleigh. When the sleigh reached home, we went to help him out, but there he had fallen over like a bag, and there he lay stone dead, and it took all our strength to lift him out of the sleigh. And his lady has sent me, saying: 'Tell the shoemaker of whom your barin just ordered boots from which he left with him—tell him that the boots are not needed, and that he is to make a pair of slippers for the corpse out of that leather just as quick as possible.' And I was to wait till they were made, and take them home with me. And so I have come."

Mikhaïla took the rest of the leather from the table and rolled it up; he also took the slippers which were all done, slapped them together, wiped them with his apron, and gave them to the young man. The young man took them.

"Good-bye, friends! Good luck to you!"

❈ ❈ ❈

Still another year, and then two more passed by, and Mikhaïla had now been living five years with Semyon. He lived in just the same way as before. He never went anywhere, he kept his own counsels, and in all that time he smiled only twice—once when Matriona gave him something to eat, and the time when he smiled on the barin.

Semyon was more than contented with his workman, and he no longer asked him where he came from; his only fear was lest Mikhaïla should leave him.

One time they were all at home. The mother was putting the iron kettles on the oven, and the children were playing on the benches and looking out of the window. Semyon was pegging away at one window, and Mikhaïla at the other was putting lifts on a heel.

One of the boys ran along the bench toward Mikhaïla, leaned over his shoulder, and looked out of the window.

"Uncle Mikhaïla, just look! A merchant's wife is coming to our house with some little girls. And one of the little girls is a cripple."

The words were scarcely out of the boy's mouth before Mikhaïla threw down his work, leaned over toward the window, and looked out-of-doors. And Semyon was surprised. Never before had Mikhaïla cared to look out, but now his face seemed soldered to the window; he was looking at something very intently.

Semyon also looked out of the window: he saw a woman coming straight through his yard; she was neatly dressed; she had two little girls by the hand; they wore shubkas [little fur garments], and kerchiefs over their heads. The little girls looked so much alike that it was hard to tell them apart, except that one of the little girls was lame in her foot; she limped as she walked.

The woman came into the entry, felt about in the dark, lifted the latch, and opened the door. She let the two little girls go before her into the cottage, and then she followed.

"How do you do, friends?"

"Welcome! What can we do for you?"

The woman sat down by the table; the two little girls clung to her knee; they were bashful.

"These little girls need to have some goatskin shoes made for the spring."

"Well, it can be done. We don't generally make such small ones; but it's perfectly easy, either with welts or lined with linen. This here is Mikhaïla; he's my master workman."

Semyon glanced at Mikhaïla, and saw that he had thrown down his work, and was sitting with his eyes fastened on the little girls.

And Semyon was amazed at Mikhaïla. To be sure the little girls were pretty; they had dark eyes, they were plump and rosy, and they wore handsome shubkas and kerchiefs; but still Semyon could not understand why he gazed so intently at them, as if they were friends of his.

Semyon was amazed, and he began to talk with the woman, and to make his bargain. After he had made his bargain, he began to take the measures. The woman lifted on her lap the little cripple, and said, "Take two measures from this one; make one little shoe from the twisted foot, and three from the well one. Their feet are alike; they are twins."

Semyon took his tape, and said in reference to the little cripple, "How did this happen to her? She is such a pretty little girl. Was she born so?"

"No; her mother crushed it."

Matriona joined the conversation; she was anxious to learn who the woman and children were, and so she said, "Then you aren't their mother?"

"No, I am not their mother; I am no relation to them, good wife, and they are no relation to me at all; I adopted them."

"If they are not your children, you take good care of them."

"Why shouldn't I take good care of them? I nursed them both at my own breast. I had a baby of my own, but God took him. I did not take such good care of him as I do these."

"Whose children are they?"

※ ※ ※

The woman became confidential, and began to tell them about it.

"Six years ago," said she, "these little ones were left orphans in one week; the father was buried on Tuesday, and the mother died on Friday. Three days these little ones remained without their father, and then their mother followed him. At that time I was living with my husband in the country: we were neighbors; we lived in adjoining yards. Their father was a peasant, and worked in the forest at woodcutting. And they were felling a tree, and it caught him across the body. It hurt him all inside. As soon as they got him out, he gave his soul to God, and that same week his wife gave birth to twins— these are the little girls here. There they were, poor and alone, no one to take care of them, either grandmother or sister.

"She must have died soon after the children were born. For when I went in the morning to look after my neighbor, as soon as I entered the cottage, I found the poor thing dead and cold. And when she died she must have rolled over on this little girl. . . . That's the way she crushed it, and spoiled this foot.

"The people got together, they washed and laid out the body, they had a coffin made, and buried her. The people were always kind. But the two little ones were left alone. What was to be done with them? Now I was the only one of the women who had a baby. For eight weeks I had been nursing my firstborn, a boy. So I took them for the time being. The peasants got together; they planned and planned what to do with them, and they said to me, 'Marya, you just keep the little girls for a while, and give us a chance to decide.'

"So I nursed the well one for a while, but did not think it worth while to nurse the deformed one. I did not expect that she was going to live. And, then, I thought to myself, why should the little angel's soul pass away? and I felt sorry for it. I tried to nurse her, and so I had my own and these two besides; yes, I had three children at the breast. But I was young and strong, and I had good food! And God gave me so much milk in my breasts that I had enough and to spare. I used to nurse two at once and let the third one wait. When one had finished, I would take up the third. And so God let me nurse all three; but when my boy was in his third year, I lost him. And God never gave me any more children. But we began to be in comfortable circumstances. And now we are living with the trader at the mill. We get good wages and live well. But we have no children of our own. And how lonely it would be, if it were not for these two little girls! How could I help loving them? They are to me like the wax in the candle!"

And the woman pressed the little lame girl to her with one arm, and with the other hand she tried to wipe the tears from her cheeks.

And Matriona sighed, and said, "The old saw isn't far wrong, 'Men can live without father and mother, but without God one cannot live.'"

While they were thus talking together, suddenly a flash of lightning seemed to irradiate from that corner of the cottage where Mikhaïla was sitting. All looked at him; and behold! Mikhaïla was sitting there with his hands folded in his lap, and looking up and smiling.

※ ※ ※

The woman went away with the children, and Mikhaïla arose from the bench and laid down his work; he took off his apron, made a low bow to the shoemaker and his wife, and said, "Farewell, friends; God has forgiven me. Do you also forgive me?"

And Semyon and Matriona perceived that it was from Mikhaïla that the light had flashed. And Semyon arose, bowed low before Mikhaïla, and said to him, "I see,

Mikhaïla, that you are not a mere man, and I have no right to detain you nor to ask questions of you. But tell me one thing: when I had found you and brought you home, you were sad; but when my wife gave you something to eat, you smiled on her, and after that you became more cheerful. And then when the barin ordered the boots, why did you smile a second time, and after that become still more cheerful; and now when this woman brought these two little girls, why did you smile for the third time and become perfectly radiant? Tell me, Mikhaïla, why was it that such a light streamed from you, and why you smiled three times?"

And Mikhaïla said, "The light blazed from me because I had been punished, but now God has forgiven me. And I smiled the three times because it was required of me to learn three of God's truths, and I have now learned the three truths of God. One truth I learned when your wife had pity on me, and so I smiled; the second truth I learned when the rich man ordered the boots, and I smiled for the second time; and now that I have seen the little girls, I have learned the third and last truth, and I smiled for the third time."

And Semyon said, "Tell me, Mikhaïla, why God punished you, and what were the truths of God, that I, too, may know them."

And Mikhaïla said, "God punished me because I disobeyed Him. I was an angel in heaven, and I was disobedient to God. I was an angel in heaven, and the Lord sent me to bring back the soul of a certain woman. I flew down to earth and I saw the woman lying alone—she was sick—she had just borne twins, two little girls. The little ones were sprawling about near their mother, but their mother was unable to lift them to her breast. The mother saw me; she perceived that God had sent me after her soul; she burst into tears, and said, 'Angel of God, I have just buried my husband; a tree fell on him in the forest and killed him. I have no sister, nor aunt, nor mother to take care of my little ones; do not carry off my soul; let me bring up my children myself, and nurse them and put them on their feet. It is impossible for children to live without father or mother.'

"And I heeded what the mother said; I put one child to her breast, and laid the other in its mother's arms, and I returned to the Lord in heaven. I flew back to the Lord, and I said, 'I cannot take the mother's soul. The father has been killed by a tree, the mother has given birth to twins, and begs me not to take her soul; she says, "Let me bring up my little ones; let me nurse them and put them on their feet. It is impossible for children to live without father and mother." I did not take the mother's soul.'

"And the Lord said, 'Go and take the mother's soul, and thou shalt learn three lessons: Thou shalt learn *what is in men,* and *what is not given unto men,* and *what men live by.* When thou shalt have learned these three lessons, then return to heaven.'

"And I flew down to earth and took the mother's soul. The little ones fell from her bosom. The dead body rolled over on the bed, and fell on one of the little girls and crushed her foot. I rose above the village and was going to give the soul to God, when a wind seized me, my wings ceased to move and fell off, and the soul arose alone to God, and I fell back to earth."

❋ ❋ ❋

And Semyon and Matriona now knew whom they had clothed and fed, and who it was that had been living with them, and they burst into tears of dismay and joy; and the angel said, "I was there in the field naked and alone. Hitherto I had never known what human poverty was; I had known neither cold nor hunger, and now I was a man. I was famished, I was freezing, and I knew not what to do. And I saw across the field a chapel made for God's service. I went to God's chapel, thinking to get shelter in it. But the chapel was locked, and I could not enter. And I crouched down behind the chapel, so as to get shelter from the wind. Evening came; I was hungry and chill, and ached all over. Suddenly I hear a man walking along the road, with a pair of boots in his hand, and talking to himself. I now saw for the first time since I had become a man the face of a mortal man, and it filled me with dismay, and I tried to hide from him. And I heard this man asking himself how he should protect himself from cold during the winter, and how he should get food for his wife and children.

"And I thought, 'I am perishing with cold and hunger, and here is a man whose sole thought is to get a shuba for himself and his wife and to furnish bread for their sustenance. It is impossible for him to help me.'

"The man saw me and scowled; he seemed even more terrible than before; then he passed on. And I was in despair. Suddenly I heard the man coming back. I looked up, and did not recognize that it was the same man as before; then there was death in his face, but now it had suddenly become alive, and I saw that God was in his face. He came to me, put clothes on me, and took me home with him.

"When I reached his house, a woman came out to meet us, and she began to scold. The woman was even more terrible to me than the man; a dead soul seemed to proceed forth from her mouth, and I was suffocated by the stench of death. She wanted to drive me out into the cold, and I knew that she would die if she drove me out. And suddenly her husband reminded her of God. And instantly a change came over the woman. And when she had prepared something for me to eat, and looked kindly on me, I looked at her, and there was no longer anything like death about her; she was now alive, and in her also I recognized God.

"And I remembered God's first lesson: *Thou shalt learn what is in men.*'

"And I perceived that *Love* was in men. And I was glad because God had begun to fulfill His promise to me, and I smiled for the first time. But I was not yet ready to know the whole. I could not understand what was not given to men, and what men lived by.

"I began to live in your house, and after I had lived with you a year the man came to order the boots which should be strong enough to last him a year without ripping or wearing out of shape. And I looked at him, and suddenly perceived behind his back my comrade, the Angel of Death. No one besides myself saw this angel; but I knew him, and I knew that before the sun should go down he would take the rich man's soul. And I said to myself; 'This man is laying his plans to live another year, and he knows not that ere evening comes he will be dead.'

"And I realized suddenly the second saying of God: *Thou shalt know what is not given unto men.*'

"And now I knew what was in men. And now I knew also what was not given unto men. It is not given unto men to know what is needed for their bodies. And I smiled for the second time. I was glad because I saw my comrade, the angel, and because God had revealed unto me the second truth.

"But I could not yet understand all. I could not understand what men live by, and so I lived on, and waited until God should reveal to me the third truth also. And now in the sixth year the little twin girls have come with the woman, and I recognized the little ones, and I remembered how they had been left.

"And after I had recognized them, I thought, 'The mother besought me in behalf of her children, because she thought that it would be impossible for children to live without father and mother, but another woman, a stranger, has nursed them and brought them up.'

"And when the woman caressed the children that were not her own, and wept over them, then I saw in her the Living God, and knew *what people live by*. And I knew that God had revealed to me the last truth, and had pardoned me, and I smiled for the third time."

❋ ❋ ❋

And the angel's body became manifest, and he was clad with light so bright that the eyes could not endure to look on him, and he spoke in clearer accents, as if the voice proceeded not from him, but came from heaven.

And the angel said, "I have learned that every man lives, not through care of himself, but by love.

"It was not given to the mother to know what her children needed to keep them alive. It was not given the rich man to know what he himself needed, and it is not given to any man to know whether he will need boots for daily living, or slippers for his burial.

"When I became a man, I was kept alive, not by what thought I took for myself, but because a stranger and his wife had love in their hearts, and pitied and loved me. The orphans were kept alive, not because other people deliberated about what was to be done with them, but because a strange woman had love for them in her heart, and pitied them and loved them. And all men are kept alive, not by their own forethought, but because there is *love in men.*

"I knew before that God gave life to men, and desired them to live; but now I know something above and beyond that.

"I have learned that God does not wish men to live each for himself, and therefore He has not revealed to them what they each need for themselves, but He wishes them to live in union, and therefore He has revealed to them what is necessary for each and for all together.

"I have now learned that it is only in appearance that they are kept alive through care for themselves, but that in reality they are kept alive through love. *He who dwelleth in love dwelleth in God, and God in him, for God is love.*"

And the angel sang a hymn of praise to God, and the cottage shook with the sound of his voice.

And the ceiling parted, and a column of fire reached from earth to heaven. And Semyon and his wife and children fell prostrate on the ground. And pinions appeared on the angel's shoulders, and he soared away to heaven.

And when Semyon opened his eyes, the cottage was the same as it had ever been, and there was no one in it save himself and his family.